The Anti-Test Anxiety SOCIETY

D0118200

published by

National Center for Youth Issues

Practical Guidance Resources
Educators Can Trust

ncyi.org

www.ncyi.org

To Doughy with love!

Forward

Test anxiety is a problem that nearly everyone experiences at one time or another. The fears of "I just can't !" or "What if I don't?" overtake confidence, and potential is instantly affected. The Anti-Test Anxiety Society is a fun story that presents 12 test taking strategies (The Dynamic Dozen) that are hands-on and easy to apply. My hope for this book is that it teaches kids of all ages how to build their test taking confidence and demonstrate their true abilities. – Julia

P.S. Doesn't it feel great to say, "Yes, I can!"

Duplication and Copyright

National Center for Youth Issues
Practical Guidance Resources
Educators Can Trust
ncyi.org

P.O. Box 22185
Chattanooga, TN 37422-2185
423.899.5714 • 800.477.8277
fax: 423.899.4547 • www.ncyi.org

ISBN: 978-1-937870-30-0
© 2014 National Center for Youth Issues, Chattanooga, TN
All rights reserved.
Written by: Julia Cook
Illustrations by: Anita DuFalla
Design by: Phillip W. Rodgers
Contributing Editor: Beth Spencer Rabon
Published by National Center for Youth Issues • Softcover
Printed at Starkey Printing, Chattanooga, Tennessee, U.S.A., July 2014

My name is
Bertha Billingsworth,
but everyone calls me

"BB"

for short.

3

I'm a pretty happy person. I have a great family.
I have a lot of friends (and some of them aren't
even human.) I like school...most of the time,
and this year, I have the BEST teacher EVER!

But I absolutely cannot stand to take tests…of any kind!

To me, the word test stands for

"Terrible Every Single Time"

because that's how
I always do on them…

TERRIBLE!

Whenever I see or
hear the word test...

The hair on the back
of my neck stands up.

My face turns as
red as a beet.

I start to sweat,
my stomach aches, and
I can't control my feet!

What if I get every answer **wrong**?
And I don't get any **right**.

I just know I'll get a bad
grade on this test,

so I don't even want to try!

My mom and dad say that I'm going to have to keep taking tests of one kind or another for the rest of my life!

But now, it seems like every time I turn around, I have to take another test. We have spelling tests every week, math tests every chapter, social studies tests every unit, and then there's the BST!

The **BIG** STATE TEST!

The big one, that really, really counts, even though we don't get graded on it.

Last week, I studied my spelling words every single night after school. I knew all of them by Tuesday, but I kept studying anyway.

Then, on Friday, when I heard my teacher say:

"Ok, it's time to take your spelling test."

The hair on the back of my neck stood up.

My face turned as red as a beet.

I started to sweat,
my stomach ached,

and I couldn't
control my feet!

What if I spell every word wrong?

And I don't get any right.

I just know I'll get a bad grade
on this test,

**so I don't even
want to try!**

10

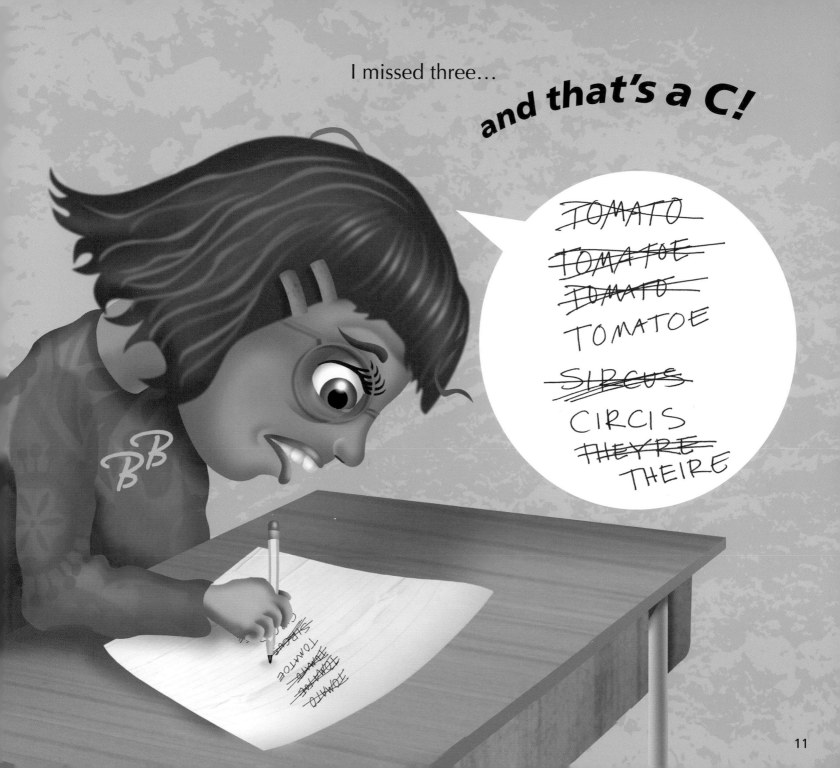

That same day, I had a math test. I knew how to do everything on it, but when I read the word **TEST** at the top of my paper…

The hair on the back of my neck stood up.

My face turned as red as a beet.

I started to sweat, my stomach ached, and I couldn't control my feet!

*What if I get every answer **wrong**?*

*And I don't get any **right**.*

I just know I'll get a bad grade on this test,

so I don't even want to try!

I missed four…

and that's a **HORRIBLE** score!

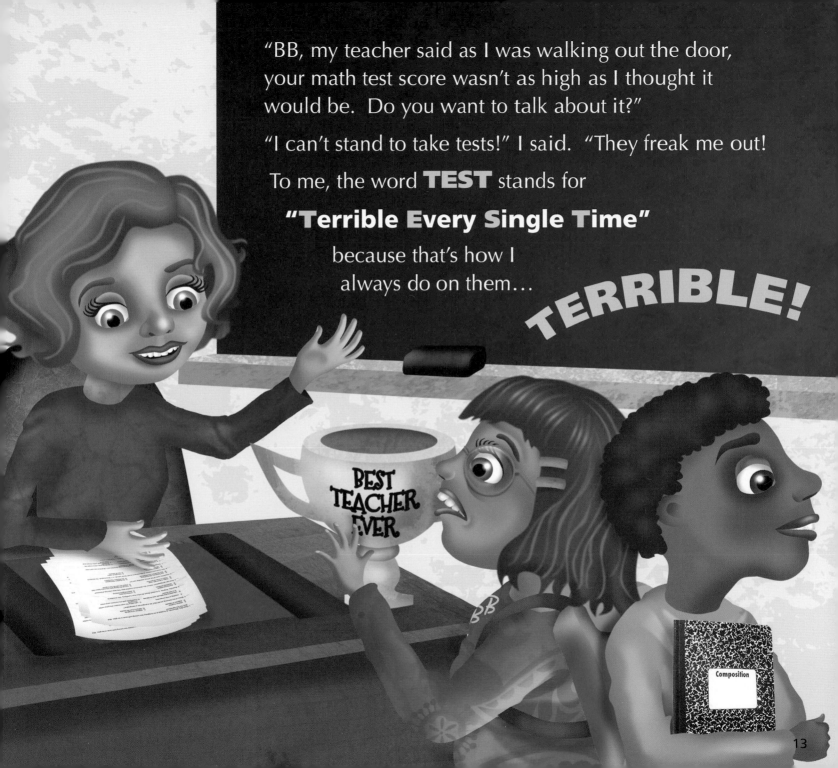

"BB, my teacher said as I was walking out the door, your math test score wasn't as high as I thought it would be. Do you want to talk about it?"

"I can't stand to take tests!" I said. "They freak me out!

To me, the word **TEST** stands for

"Terrible Every Single Time"

because that's how I
always do on them...

TERRIBLE!

"Sounds like you need to become a member of the **Anti-Test Anxiety Society** (that's ATAS for short!")

"What's that?"

"The Anti-Test Anxiety Society" is a very special club.

It's full of kids who believe that they "CAN."

Kids that show what they're made of!"

"If you can prepare the right way when you need to take a test, when the test comes along, you'll believe that you CAN, and then you CAN do your best."

"Test doesn't stand for "Terrible Every Single Time." You know deep down that's not true. Instead, make the letters in the word TEST, stand for "Think Each Situation Through!"

ATAS

ATAS

"But how do I do that?"

"First of all, you need to start using the **GET TO** part of your brain instead of the **HAVE TO** part of your brain."

"My what?"

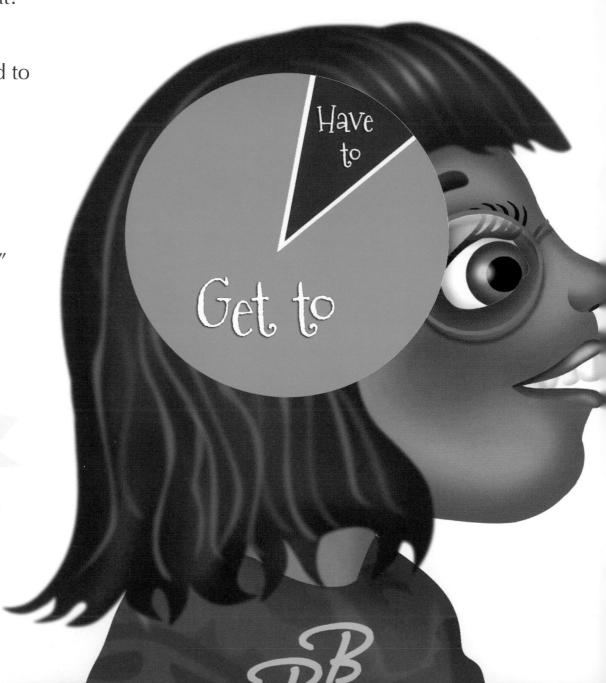

"Your brain has two parts: the **GET TO** and the **HAVE TO**,
but one is much bigger in size.

When you **GET TO** do something instead of **HAVE TO**,
your brain fills up with **TRY!**

"If you tell yourself you **HAVE TO** take a test, you might be setting yourself up to fail.

Instead, if you think I **GET TO** take a test, you'll have a better chance of doing well.

GET TO, **HAVE TO**, **GET TO**, **HAVE TO**…It's your choice which one to choose.

Try using your **GET TO** brain a lot more…

What do you have to lose?"

"Using your GET TO brain is the key to opening the door to good test preparation."

"What's that?"

"A good test taker needs to prepare in order to do well on a test.

If you will do just 12 simple things, you won't have near as much stress."

"These 12 simple things, called the

DYNAMIC DOZEN,

will lessen your test anxiety.

If you will do them, you can become a member of our great society!"

Test Preparation

"Here's the list:

1. Tell yourself you **CAN** do well. **TEST** stands for "**T**hink **E**ach **S**ituation **T**hrough." You get to show how much you have learned when you take a test…lucky you! And I get to see how much I have taught you… lucky me!!!

2. Don't cram…It's hard on your brain! Instead, spread out your studying time over a few days or weeks. Practice doing sample problems, and look over your class material every day until you take the test.

3. When you study, draw a picture of what you are learning inside your head.

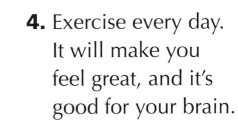

Order of Operations
Please - ( )
Excuse - Exponents
My - Multiplication
Ditzy - Division
Aunt - Addition
Sally - Subtraction

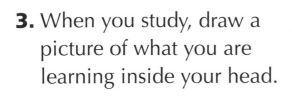

4. Exercise every day. It will make you feel great, and it's good for your brain.

5. Get a good night's sleep the night before your test so your brain and body aren't tired and worn out.

6. Stay relaxed. If you start to stress out right before a test, close your eyes, take a few deep breaths and go on a mini-mental vacation. Think about your happiest place, and let your mind go there for a few minutes…

Just don't forget to come back!

7. Read the directions slowly and carefully, and if you don't understand what they say, ask your teacher to explain them to you.

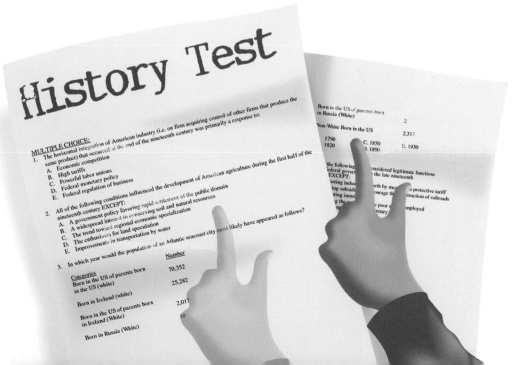

8. Skim through the test so you know how long it is. Then you won't spend too much time on any one question.

9. Write down the important stuff that you need to memorize (formulas, facts, definitions, etc.) at the top or on the side of your test paper so they don't clog up your brain and you don't forget to use them.

The provinces and territories of Canada combine to make up the world's second-largest country by area. The three territories are Northwest Territories, Nunavut, and Yukon.

Geography Test

1.____ A Prairie province which has a drainage divide line for its south west border.
2.____ A Canadian territory which has a line of latitude, a line of longitude and a drainage divide line for borders.
3.____ Canada's newest territory.
4.____ Manitoba
5.____ Quebec
6.____ A Prairie province whose borders are entirely lines of latitude and longitude.
7.____ Canada's furthest province west.
8.____ The position of Lake Superior.
9.____ The North Saskatchewan River empties here.
10.____ The Mackenzie River empties here.
11.____ Canada's southernmost point.
12.____ A Maritime province which is a peninsula.
13.____ An island Maritime province.
14.____ The Atlantic Ocean.
15.____ A line of latitude which separates Canada's provinces from its territories.
16.____ Canada's capital city is in this Canadian Shield province.
17.____ The divide line for rivers that run into the Pacific Ocean, the Hudson Bay and the Arctic Ocean.
18.____ The Yukon
19.____ The line of latitude dividing Canada and the USA.
20.____ Baffin Island

21.____ Place an X on the North Pole
22.____ Place a Z on the Hudson Bay
23.____ Place a T on Greenland
24.____ Darken the line of latitude which you think is the Equator
25.____ Circle the Great Lakes
26.____ Label the USA
27.____ Label South America
____ Label the Atlantic Ocean

10. Do the easy questions first to build up your confidence. Then, you will have more time to work on the harder ones.

EASY First

HARD Last

Literal means
- ☐ Actual
- ~~☐ Without lit~~
- ☐ In a factual manner
- ~~☐ From Lithuania~~

11. On multiple choice tests, cross out answers that don't make sense so you can narrow down your choices.

12. Check a random 5:

Pick any five questions, and recheck your answers. If you have time, recheck five more.

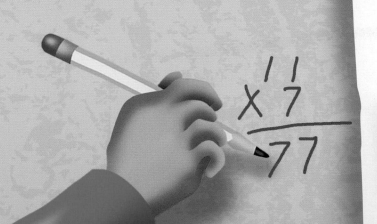

$$\overset{1\,1}{\times 7} \over 77$$

Math Test, Unit 7

$33 \div 3 \quad 11$

$40 \div 4 \quad 10$

42×7
294

$$5\overline{)530} \atop \begin{array}{r} 106 \\ \underline{5} \\ 30 \\ \end{array}$$

$$7\overline{)77} \atop \begin{array}{r} 11 \\ \underline{7} \\ 7 \end{array}$$

$$\begin{array}{r} 23 \\ \times 2 \\ \hline 46 \end{array} \quad \begin{array}{r} 12 \\ \times 8 \\ \hline 96 \end{array} \quad \begin{array}{r} ^{2}34 \\ \times 7 \\ \hline 238 \end{array}$$

I listened to everything my teacher told me and most of it made quite a bit of sense, so I decided to give it a try.

First of all, I switched over from using my **HAVE TO** brain to using my **GET TO** brain, and for the past few weeks, I've really tried hard to do all 12 things…I actually think it might be working!

Now whenever I take a test:

The hair on the back of my neck stays down,
and my face doesn't look like a beet.

I don't sweat anymore,
my stomach feels fine,
and I CAN control my feet!

Today I aced my spelling test, and
I only missed one on my math.

I'm getting an A in Social Studies,
and school's an absolute **BLAST!**

Before I tried the

DYNAMIC DOZEN,

I was filled to the
top with anxiety.

But now I'm an
official member of the

ATA SOCIETY.

OFFICIAL
MEMBER
ATAS

To me, the word *TEST* used to stand for

"Terrible Every Single Time,"

But I'm changing the Terrible to Terrific,

and I'm feeling mighty fine!

P.S. Hopefully, this ATA stuff
will work on the BST…

even though it's not graded!

Ease Your Test Stress
with the
DYNAMIC DOZEN!

1. Tell yourself you **CAN** do well. **TEST** stands for "**Think Each Situation Through**." You get to show how much you have learned when you take a test…lucky you! And I get to see how much I have taught you… lucky me!!!

2. Don't cram…It's hard on your brain! Instead, spread out your studying time over a few days or weeks. Practice doing sample problems, and look over your class material every day until you take the test.

3. When you study, draw a picture of what you are learning inside your head.

4. Exercise every day. It will make you feel great, and it's good for your brain.

5. Get a good night's sleep the night before your test so your brain and body aren't tired and worn out.

6. Stay relaxed. If you start to stress out right before a test, close your eyes, take a few deep breaths and go on a mini-mental vacation. Think about your happiest place, and let your mind go there for a few minutes…just don't forget to come back!

7. Read the directions slowly and carefully, and if you don't understand what they say, ask your teacher to explain them to you.

8. Skim through the test so you know how long it is. Then you won't spend too much time on any one question.

9. Write down the important stuff that you need to memorize (formulas, facts, definitions, etc.) at the top or on the side of your test paper so they don't clog up your brain and you don't forget to use them.

10. Do the easy questions first to build up your confidence. Then, you will have more time to work on the harder ones.

11. On multiple choice tests, cross out answers that don't make sense so you can narrow down your choices.

12. Check a random 5: Pick any five questions, and recheck your answers. If you have time, recheck five more.

OFFICIAL MEMBER
ATAS